D0624846

CALGARY PUBLIC LIBRARY

SEP - - 2009

This book belongs to

_____

The Bunnies'

by Lezlie Evans

For Jordan, Whitney, Cameron,
Christian, and Brennan—my five bunny brothers—L.E.

For the four little bunnies in my life,
Katie, Jameson, Malcolm, and Sadie—K.C.

Picnic

illustrations by Kay Chorao

HYPERION BOOKS FOR CHILDREN
NEW YORK

Text © 2007 Lezlie Evans   Illustrations © 2007 by Kay Sproat Chorao   All rights reserved.

Printed in Singapore   First Edition   10 9 8 7 6 5 4 3 2 1   Library of Congress Cataloging-in-Publication Data on file.

ISBN 0-7868-1612-0   Reinforced binding   Visit www.hyperionbooksforchildren.com

Bunny one and bunny two
get ready to make yummy stew.

Bunny three and bunny four
go grab the baskets by the door.

Bunny five and bunny six
start on their way with walking sticks.

Bunny seven and bunny eight
bounce down the path and through the gate.

The bunnies quick begin to pick,
and in their baskets they each stick
some pumpkin heads and ears of corn.

Abundant vegetables adorn
the countryside and gardens, too:
ingredients for bunnies' stew.

With baskets packed and neatly stacked,

the bunnies eight then bounce right back.

See bunnies peeling, bunnies chopping

vegetables that go plip-plopping.

A sweet aroma, so enticing,
fills the air as they are dicing.
Here are carrots, beans, and peas.

Add more potatoes, if you please.
Then sprinkle herbs and shake the salt
until one bunny hollers … "Halt!"

HALT

Bunny one and bunny two
are balancing the pot of stew.
Bunny three and bunny four
shout, "Watch the peelings on the floor!"

Bunny five and bunny six
say, "Looks like acrobatic tricks."

Bunny seven and bunny eight
reach out to help, but they're too late!

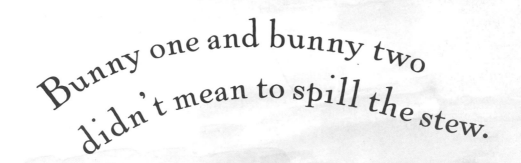

Bunny one and bunny two
didn't mean to spill the stew.

Bunny three and bunny four
help clean the mess up off the floor.

Bunny five and bunny six
recover only two small licks.
Bunny seven and bunny eight
have grumbling tummies, but must wait.

What a blue bunny crew.
It took all day to make that stew.

These bunnies need their problem solved,
so every bunny gets involved.

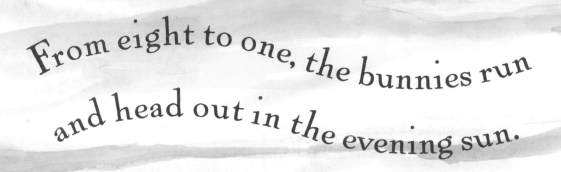

From eight to one, the bunnies run and head out in the evening sun.

The bunnies look, and soon they find crisp, leafy greens of every kind.

With squash and spice, mushrooms are nice.
Three ripe tomatoes will suffice.

Four bunnies toss, four bunnies mix.
And what a grand feast all eight fix!

"Some for me and some for you," says bunny one to bunny two.

Bunny three and bunny four say, "Pass us seconds. We'd like more."

Bunny five and bunny six
shout, "Hooray for night picnics!"

All the bunnies, one through eight, think the day turned out first-rate!

The End